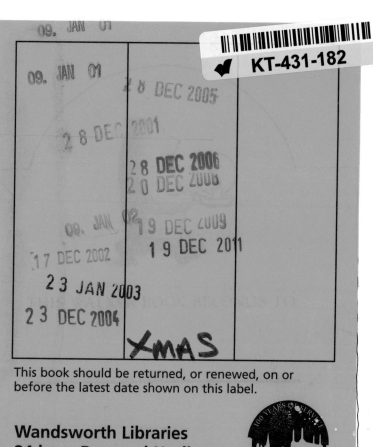

For Clare – a star! With love from Viv
For Caera Rose A.Y.G

First published 1997
by Walker Books Ltd
87 Vauxhall Walk
London SE11 5HJ

This edition published 2000

2 4 6 8 10 9 7 5 3 1

Text © 1997 Vivian French
Illustrations © 1997 Anne Yvonne Gilbert

This book has been typeset in M Garamond.

Printed in Hong Kong

British Library Cataloguing in Publication Data
A catalogue record for this book
is available from the British Library.

ISBN 0-7445-7845-0

A Christmas Star Called Hannah

Vivian French

illustrated by

Anne Yvonne Gilbert

WALKER BOOKS

AND SUBSIDIARIES

LONDON • BOSTON • SYDNEY

"Come on, Mum," said Hannah, "or we'll be late for school."
"We're just coming," Mum said, tucking Paul into his buggy.
Hannah gave a little skip.
"Mrs Hill's going to tell us about a surprise today – a Christmas surprise. I think it might be iced biscuits."
"That's nice," said Mum.

Mrs Hill called all the children together
at story time.
"Now," said Mrs Hill, "we're going to put
on a Christmas play for our mums and dads
and friends. We're going to tell them the
story of Mary and Joseph and the
baby Jesus."
"Hurrah!" said Hannah.

Everyone was told who or what they would be. Hannah was cross because Mrs Hill chose Zak to be Joseph and Susie to be Mary. Hannah was only a star. She went to sit under the table. "This is a very special star," Mrs Hill told her. "You'll show everyone the way to the stable."

"Policemen do that," Hannah said. "Stars just twinkle."

Mrs Hill sighed. "This star is baby Jesus' very own star."

"Oh." Hannah thought about stars for a moment.

"I'll be a star, then," she said.

Zak's mum came to help the children paint
a big picture of the inn and the stable where
the baby Jesus was born. Susie and Roger
and Ataf went to look in the playhouse for
a doll to be the baby. Hannah came over
to see what they were doing.
"I could bring my dolly from home,"
she said. "It's much bigger than this one."
"Oh, I think this one will do, Hannah,"
said Zak's mum.

Hannah went over to the dressing-up corner.
She put on a big hat, some shiny beads and
a pair of sparkly shoes.
"I've found some things to wear," she said.
"Look!"
Roger's mum looked at her list of names.
"Aren't you the Christmas star, Hannah?"
Hannah nodded. "These are my star clothes."
"I don't think they're quite right, dear,"
Roger's mum said. "We're going to make you
a lovely sparkly costume."
"Can't I wear the hat I found?" Hannah asked.
"No, dear," said Roger's mum.

Hannah walked home very slowly.
"I don't want to be in the play," she said.
"Plays are horrid."
"It'll be fun when you do it," said her mum.
"Paul and I are both coming to watch."
"I expect Paul will cry and spoil it,"
Hannah said crossly.

On the day of the play all the mums and dads and friends packed into the hall. The children put on their costumes and peeped out through the curtains.

"I can see my mum and Paul," said Hannah.

"Is everybody ready?" Mrs Hill asked. "Susie, have you got the doll wrapped up, ready to be baby Jesus?"

Susie stared at Mrs Hill. Then she began to cry.

"I've forgotten it," she sobbed.

Jamie's dad began to play the piano.
"We'll have to pretend that we've got a baby Jesus," Mrs Hill said, quickly wiping Susie's nose. "Don't cry, Susie."
"I know what!" Hannah jumped down from her bench. "I've got a baby to be Jesus!"
She burst through the curtains and rushed down the hall. A moment later she was back, pushing Paul in his baby buggy.
"There," Hannah said proudly, "now we've got a *real* baby!"

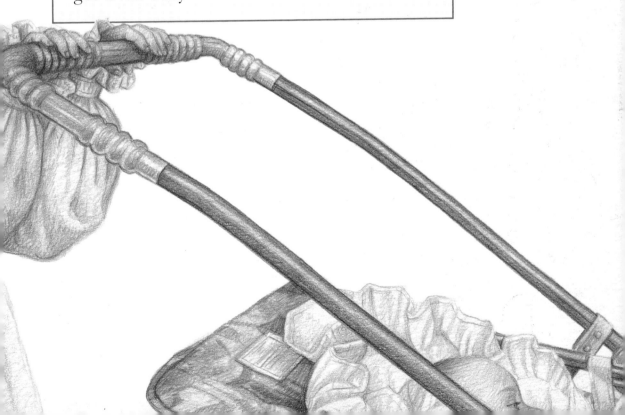

Mrs Hill looked very anxious, but Mary and Joseph were already pushing the buggy carefully across the stage to the stable. Roger's mum pulled the curtains wide open, and Hannah stood high up on her bench and shone happily over Paul.

At the end, everyone clapped and clapped and said it was the best play ever. Mrs Hill gave Hannah a big hug.

"Well done, Hannah," she said, "your baby was lovely."

Hannah climbed down from her bench.

"I was a very special Christmas star, wasn't I?" she said.

"Yes, dear," said Mrs Hill, "you were the best Christmas star ever!"

A Christmas Star Called Hannah

VIVIAN FRENCH says "When my daughters were little, they always wanted to be Mary in the school nativity play. Jessica was once – but Jemima was only the donkey… and she was very cross – just like Hannah!"

Vivian worked in children's theatre for ten years as both an actor and writer, before becoming an acclaimed children's author and storyteller. Her picture books include *Please, Princess Primrose!*, *A Song for Little Toad* (shortlisted for the 1995 Smarties Book Prize), a retelling of *A Christmas Carol*, *Christmas Mouse* and the non-fiction titles *Caterpillar Caterpillar* (shortlisted for the Kurt Maschler Award) and *Growing Frogs*. She has also written many fiction titles for young readers. She lives in Bristol.

YVONNE GILBERT says that "Hannah is actually my niece Caera, and everyone else in the pictures is either a friend or a relative. The picture where Hannah is under the table was the most difficult for Caera to pose for – she either could not or would not remember what she looked like when she was being naughty!"

Yvonne works as a photographer as well as an illustrator. She has illustrated several books and numerous book covers. She lives in Northumberland with her son Thomas, who she says is often "the star" of her books.

ISBN 0-7445-6021-7 (pb)

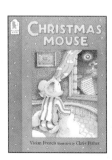
ISBN 0-7445-7212-6 (pb)

ISBN 0-7445-5299-0 (pb)

ISBN 0-7445-6941-9 (pb)